FATED TO THE DOCTOR

ASPEN RIDGE PACK: SHIFTER M.D.
BOOK 3

LUNA WILDER

WANT A FREE BOOK?

Want a free copy of Wolf Lover? It's a steamy, scarred military hero, curvy girl romance! Check it out today here!

*

Can he handle another heartbreak?

Micah Davis has always been a lone wolf.

His parents passed when he was younger, and he was the oddball in his pack.

Now that he's back from medical school, he's looking forward to focusing on his career and nothing else.

Then he walks into Aspen Ridge Medical and locks eyes with Kaia Luxe, and his carefully laid plans go up in smoke.

She's accident-prone, and he's afraid to lose another loved one, but he can't resist her.

They're fated to be, but will Micah claim her or is he still convinced that he would be better off alone?

ONE

Kaia

"I THOUGHT this trail was supposed to be easy," I wheeze as I follow my best friend, Kingsley, up the dirt path.

"It said easy," she says, but she doesn't sound so sure.

She's breathing just as hard as I am, and I wonder if I can convince her to turn back yet. Going on this hike was her idea, and I thought it would be a great way to check out some of the views here in Alaska, but all I've seen so far is some melting snow and trees.

"It's probably the change in altitude," I pant, and she giggles.

"That and the fact that we've been sitting on our butts for the last four years, studying," she adds, and I laugh.

"That *may* have something to do with it, too," I agree.

"I think that we're almost to the top," she says, and I try to focus on that as we walk up the last stretch of trail.

Kingsley and I just graduated from college two weeks ago, and we're on one last trip before we get settled into the next chapter of our lives. We've been best friends basically since birth, and we've spent every break and vacation since we were sixteen visiting new places.

Our dream was to see all fifty states and then travel the rest of the world. We've managed to do forty-eight of them in the last six years. All that was left was Hawaii and Alaska. We're in Alaska now, and we'll be here for the next week before we fly out to Hawaii.

We've already hit up the major cities here, and now we're in this quiet town in the middle of the wilderness. It's beautiful out here, and part of me never wants to leave.

"Whoa," Kingsley breathes out, and this time it's not even because she's out of breath.

Or at least not entirely because she's out of breath.

"I sure could get used to that view," I say, and she nods.

We stare out over the vast wilderness, marveling at the view of mountains and forests. It looks like a postcard, and I wish I was better with a camera and could capture this.

"Alright, this might have been worth the hike," I say, and she laughs.

"We still have to walk back down."

"Maybe not," I retort, and she laughs harder.

"We can take turns carrying each other."

"Deal," I say, linking my arm with hers.

It's starting to get dark, so we can't stay and marvel at the views for much longer.

"I'm starving."

"I know, but we ate all the snacks on the way up here. The hike back down will probably go faster, right?" She asks, and I shrug.

"Let's go."

Kingsley and I have always been thick as thieves. We grew up together and maybe that's why we're so close, even though we couldn't be more different. She's my complete opposite in so many ways. I'm more of a dreamer, while she's a realist. I tend to have big plans, and she helps to ground me. Somehow, our differences just mesh perfectly together. She's the sister that I never had.

Our parents are close too. In fact, they still vacation together. They're currently in Thailand. They had offered to take us with them, but Kingsley and I were set on finishing our bucket list instead.

The sun is starting to set fast now as we trek back down. We're joking and laughing together. Kingsley keeps close to my side, and I know she's worried about me tripping and falling again. My jeans are still covered in dirt from when I stumbled on the hike up.

I've always been clumsy. I seem to trip or bump into something at least once a day. I know it's because I have a hard time concentrating on my surroundings, especially when I'm excited about something else.

Kingsley and my family are all used to seeing me with bruises and bandages. She hadn't even blinked an eye when I tripped earlier. Instead, she just helped me up and made sure that I was alright. My parents have had my eyes tested, but they were always fine. I've been tested for ADHD and a handful of other conditions, but I never had them. I'm just spacey and clumsy.

Kingsley points over to our left, and I glance at the fox that's skittering away from us.

"He's so cute!" I say, and that's when it happens.

I feel myself start to fall forward, and I gasp, my arms shooting out to brace my fall, but it's too late. Pain shoots up my arm from my wrist, and I wince, cradling my wrist against my chest.

"Kaia!" Kingsley cries out, and I roll over onto my butt to look up at her.

"I'm okay. It's probably just bruised. Maybe sprained," I tell her.

I would know. I've had more sprains, fractures, and broken bones than I'd care to remember. It doesn't feel broken, and there are no bones poking out, so I doubt that it's broken.

"We should still go to the hospital and have it checked out," Kingsley says as she helps me up to my feet.

"I think I could just ice it," I say, and she shakes her head.

"No, let's go get it checked out. Otherwise, I'm going to be worried about you for the rest of the trip. I doubt that the wait will be long. The town isn't that big," she says, and I sigh.

"Alright, but then we go back to the hotel room and binge eat all of the carbs we can find," I counter, and she grins.

"Duh."

We're almost to the bottom of the trail, and Kingsley gets the passenger door for me.

"Thanks."

She nods, making sure that I'm settled before she heads over to the driver's side. She climbs behind the wheel, and we take off toward downtown Aspen Ridge.

We looked around town a bit when we got here yesterday but didn't explore that much. We'll have to come check out the little shops lining the streets in town tomorrow.

The hospital comes into view, and my stomach growls as we park in a spot near the front door.

"I'll get you settled, and then go find us some food while we wait," Kingsley says as we climb out.

"I can go in if you want to leave now," I offer.

"It's fine. I'm sure that there's a vending machine inside. Maybe they'll bring you back right away, and we'll be in and out soon. We can try to hit up one of the restaurants we just passed."

I follow Kingsley inside, and she heads up to the front desk. I glance up, and my eyes lock on the hottest man I've ever seen. His dark brown hair is tousled like he's been running his hands through it a lot. He's tall, well over six feet, with an athletic build.

He belongs on the cover of magazines, and I'm surprised to notice that he's wearing a white coat. I've been to a lot of doctors and hospitals in my life, and I've never had a doctor who looked like him before.

He's leaning against the reception desk, and he glances at Kingsley and then me. His gaze clashes with mine, and we stare at each other.

I can feel a flush starting to stain my cheeks, and I swallow hard as my whole body starts to overheat. I don't know what it is about this man. I've never reacted this way to anyone before. I have no experience with men. I was always so focused on school, and if I wasn't in class or studying, I was hanging out with Kingsley. She was just as disinterested in the opposite sex as I was.

My heart starts to race as I stumble forward a step, and his eyes flash as he turns to face me fully.

I don't know what is happening here, but I think I'm going to like it.

TWO

Micah

IT'S HER.

My wolf lunges, not wanting to deal with her obviously injured arm. He just wants to claim her.

I grit my teeth, holding him in check.

We're in public, I remind him, and he growls.

Take her to an exam room then and make her ours!

I clear my throat, ignoring my wolf and pasting a smile on my face as I greet my mate and her friend.

"Checking in?" I ask them, my eyes straying over to my curvy mate.

"Yeah, my friend hurt her wrist on our hike," her friend says, and I nod; my wolf and I breathing in our mate's sweet scent.

We take her in. Her pale blonde hair is half buried under her knit hat, and I watch as she pulls it off and unzips her coat, letting me take in her curves. She's wearing jeans and a purple knit sweater. She looks cozy and so inviting.

My wolf and I just want to curl up next to her, but when she winces, tightening her hold on her wrist, I blink back to the task at hand.

I take a deep breath, my mouth watering as I get more of her scent. She smells like the outdoors, but under that is an alluring scent that is all my mate. It's like roses and honey.

I lick my lips, and my wolf growls at me, begging me to bite her already. We've been arguing about our mate ever since we were eighteen. My wolf is excited to find our mate and not be alone anymore. Me, on the other hand? Not so much.

I've been on my own ever since I was eleven, and my parents were killed in a hunting accident. From then on, I was the oddball in my pack. I was like a ghost, always hanging on the fringes of the pack. Most people forgot about me, and I got used to it.

I've been taking care of myself ever since. I got used to it. My parents had left me a trust, and I used that money to go to college and then medical school. I knew once I had graduated that I didn't want to go back to my old pack, and that's when I started looking for a new place to live.

I never really saw myself in a small town, but when I got a job offer from Aspen Ridge, I kind of fell in love with the pack and area. I've found my place here at the hospital with my friends, and now I can't imagine leaving.

I pass her friend a clipboard and then smile, waving my mate over to an empty exam room. Roman comes out of the office and raises his eyebrow at me when he sees me leading my mate into the room.

It's the two of us on shift tonight, and I'm guessing he's upset that I have a patient. We've both been bored out of our minds all shift. I spent my time pacing up and down the halls, getting caught up on emails and paperwork, and then spinning around in an office chair while Roman texted his mate, Iggy.

Iggy and Roman were just mated a few months ago, and Jax met his mate, Parker, just last month. Now the two of them are both blissed out and in love. Seeing them so happy has had me rethinking my stance on never finding my mate, and now that my mate is before me, I know that I need to make my decision fast.

My wolf snarls inside me, and I grit my teeth, ignoring him.

"I'm Micah," I say as she takes a seat on the bed.

"Kaia James," she says, her green eyes shining as she looks up at me.

I wonder if her eyes would darken when I sink inside her for the first time. Would she cry out my name or just moan? My wolf starts to pace inside of me as I repeat her name in my head.

I love how it sounds. I want to say it out loud, to taste it on my lips.

Maybe I should claim my mate. Why was I so against this again?

My wolf licks his lips, and I clear my throat, trying to focus on the task at hand.

"How did you hurt your wrist?" I ask her.

"Hiking," she says with a laugh. "I tripped going down. And up," she says with another laugh as she looks down at the dirt on her jeans. "I'm a bit of a klutz."

My stomach sinks, and I swallow as her friend comes in and passes me the clipboard. I had forgotten about her, and I scan over the paperwork, taking in the list of surgeries and broken bones.

"She's quite accident-prone," her friend says, and Kaia laughs.

She's accident-prone. Taking care of her would be a full-time job. I would always be worried about her. What if she gets seriously hurt? What if she dies?

An image of me standing alone at my parents' graves flashes behind my eyes, and suddenly, I'm reminded why I never wanted to find my fated mate. I can't lose someone else, especially not someone who is so vital and important to me. I barely got over losing my parents, and I know I'll never get over losing my mate.

My wolf howls in pain inside me as I mentally take a step back from my mate. We've been at war over this topic for years, but it's different, worse, now that we've found our mate, and it's no longer just a hypothetical situation.

My wolf lunges again, and I grit my teeth, stumbling back a step. Both girls stare at me in surprise, and I clear my throat again.

"I'll... I'll be right back," I stammer out, then I turn and flee the room before they can respond.

"Whoa! Is everything okay?" Roman asks when I nearly plow him over.

I hesitate. I want to talk to someone about all of this, but I know that Roman would never understand. He doesn't know about my parents, and he never had any doubts about his mate. He was always trying to find her and was so happy when he met Iggy.

If I told him that I had just met my fated mate and wasn't sure if I wanted to claim her, he would think I was crazy. I wish Asher was here. He would understand. He knows about my parents' deaths, and he's just as opposed to finding his mate as I was to finding mine.

"Yeah, I'm fine. Just need to grab something," I lie, and he frowns but doesn't say anything as I head down the hallway.

I duck into a storage closet and close the door behind me. My heart is racing, and I take a deep breath, trying to clear up my jumbled thoughts.

My wolf is pissed inside of me, but I ignore him. I need to figure out what I want to do now and then get back to treat my mate. I can't be worried about him right now.

So, what are the facts?

I've found my mate. Now, what am I going to do about it?

Should I try to claim her? Should I pretend I didn't realize she was my mate and try to forget her? Is that even possible?

Maybe I'm blowing all this out of proportion since I was so caught off guard at finding my mate. Maybe they were exaggerating how clumsy and accident-prone she is. Maybe this is all just a miscommunication.

I need to give my mate a chance and get to know her a little bit more. Then I can make a decision on what to do now that we've found our fated mate.

My wolf isn't exactly happy with me as we head back to her room, but as long as we're going to be close to our Kaia, he seems to have calmed down.

I roll my shoulders back as I head into the room to treat my mate.

THREE

Kaia

"WHAT ARE they putting in the water up here?" Kingsley whispers to me as soon as Dr. Micah steps out of the room.

I giggle, my heart still beating out of control in my chest as I turn to face her more.

"I know, right? He's so hot."

"I think he's into you, too," she says quietly, and I can feel a blush starting to stain my cheeks.

I'm not sure that I agree with her. He keeps switching from seeming interested in me to putting up a wall. When he left, he was acting like he couldn't get away from me fast enough. His mood swings are starting to give me whiplash, and I wonder if having more experience with men in the past would have helped me out now.

Maybe I'm reading this whole situation wrong. He's probably just being friendly, and I'm just hoping it's something more.

Still, I can't help but remember the way he was staring

at me. It was like he wanted to rip my clothes off and take me right here on this hospital bed.

An image of his big body pressing mine down into the thin mattress fills my head, and I clear my throat, trying to get my mind out of the gutter.

I twist my knit hat between my fingers. I'm suddenly feeling like I'm dangerously close to overheating. Kingsley wiggles out of her coat and hat, too, and I look around the hospital room. It looks like every other hospital room I've been in, but something feels different this time. I just can't put my finger on what.

The door opens, and my spine straightens, but it's not Dr. Micah. Instead, a nurse comes bustling in. She gives me a friendly smile, and I relax.

"I'm here to take you down for some X-rays. We need to make sure that nothing is broken," she says as she pushes a wheelchair closer to the bed.

"I don't think it is," I tell her, and she smiles.

"We still have to be sure, dear," she says as I take a seat in the wheelchair. "There's no line right now, so we'll get you in and out quickly."

"I'm going to go grab us some food. I'll be here when you get back," Kingsley says, and I wave with my good hand as I'm wheeled down the hall.

Soft music plays, and I hum along under my breath as I'm wheeled down the bright, sterile hallway and into another room. I know the drill by now, and I just make small talk with the nurse, Jan, as she sets up the X-ray machine.

"How are you liking Aspen Ridge so far?" She asks me.

"I really like it. It's so pretty here. The hike was fun... until I fell," I add, and she laughs.

"Well, hopefully, nothing is broken or fractured, and

we'll get you back out on the trails in no time," Jan says, and I smile.

"I think that we're actually going to be hiking around the shops downtown tomorrow," I joke, and she laughs.

"We'll get you ready for the shops in no time," she says, and I smile as she heads behind the counter to take the X-rays.

My eyes are drawn over to the window by the door, and my breath stalls in my lungs when I see Micah standing there. He's watching me, studying me closely, and I watch him right back.

His blue eyes almost look like they're glowing, but that can't be right. It must be the lights in the hospital, and I wonder if my own green eyes are also looking illuminated.

"Just try to stay still, dear," Jan says, and I rip my eyes away from Micah to focus on her and the X-rays.

"Sorry," I say, and she waves my apology away.

"It's fine. We just need to get another angle now," Jan says as she comes over to move my arm to its side.

We take another X-ray, and I glance back at the window, but Micah is gone. It feels like there's a pit in my stomach when I realize that he left again, and I try to ignore the bereft feeling as Jan wheels me back to my room.

Kingsley is still not back, but I'm sure she will be soon. I get situated on the bed and thank Jan before she heads back out into the hall. The door closes behind her, and I relax, only to jump in my seat when the door almost immediately opens back up.

I expect it to be Kingsley, but instead, Micah walks back into the room.

"Did you get the results back already?" I ask him, and he blinks.

"What? Oh, no, not yet."

"Oh," I say as he wheels over the chair and takes a seat across from me.

"So, you have a lot of these types of accidents?" He asks, and I sag in disappointment.

I thought that maybe he was trying to show interest in me, but I guess that it's just another welfare check.

"Yeah, I've always been clumsy. My parents used to say it was because I always had my head in the clouds," I say with a smile.

"Any serious injuries?" He asks, and I notice that he seems strangely weird about me being clumsy and having accidents.

"Um, no. It's just been bruises, cuts, and broken bones."

"Good," he says, seeming to relax.

"I guess..."

"I mean, I'm glad that it's never been a life or death situation."

"Right," I say because I'm still getting the feeling that there's something more happening here.

"How long are you in Aspen Ridge?" He asks, changing the subject.

"Um, a few more days. We leave on Monday."

"Five days," he mumbles to himself, and I frown.

I want to ask him if he's okay, but he seems set on this game of twenty questions.

"Where are you from originally?"

"Grand Rapids, Michigan."

"Are you going back there?"

"Yes?"

"Do you like it there?"

"It's home. My parents are there."

"So, you wouldn't ever move then?"

"I mean, I guess I wouldn't say never. It would depend on a lot of things."

Where is this going?

"And your friend?"

"Kingsley?"

"Right. Is she from Michigan too?"

"Yeah. We've been best friends since like birth."

"What do you do for a living?"

"We just graduated from college, actually. We're looking for jobs now, but we have a social media business we've been trying to build up."

"And you can do that anywhere."

"Um, yeah."

Why is he so focused on my location?

"Good."

I frown, my mouth opening, but I'm not sure what to say back to that.

"How old are you?"

"Twenty-one."

"Are you single?"

"Yes?"

"Yes?" He asks, his tone pointed.

"Yes, I'm single. Is that a medical question?"

"No."

We stare at each other, and I want to ask him what that means, but before I can, the door opens, and Kingsley walks in, her arms full of snacks.

"All that was open was the vending machine," she says, and I smile.

"That's fine."

I look back to Micah, but he's already out of his chair and headed out the door. I watch him go, my head filled with even more questions about the handsome doctor.

FOUR

Micah

"SO, YOU JUST LET HER GO?" Jax asks, staring at me like I'm an idiot.

Roman has a similar look on his face, but Asher is nodding and staring at me knowingly.

"I panicked. I didn't know how to get her to stay, and she was with her friend," I try to argue.

"They sound close. You could have told both of them," Roman says, and I sigh.

"Well, I didn't, and now it's too late."

Asher shrugs, looking over this conversation, I know that he's not going to be any help in this situation. I turn back to Roman and Jax. They both look confused, and I know they're trying to understand how my wolf and I could stand not to claim and mark our mate.

"What do I do now?" I ask them, and they frown.

"Find her? She's still in town, right?" Jax asks.

"Yeah, for a few more days."

"Okay, so find her and ask her out on a date. That way, you two are alone, and you can explain shifters and fated mates in privacy," Roman suggests.

"You make it sound so easy. How do I ask her out? Just try to bump into her? She's going to be with her friend. What if she doesn't want to leave her alone?"

"It will only be for a few hours," Roman says, and I sigh.

"Or you could try to tell her in public. Maybe when her friend is distracted," Jax offers.

"No, that's a terrible idea. No human is just going to believe that shifters exist, and you don't want to have that conversation in public. What if she freaks out and more humans hear you?" Asher says.

"He might be right," Roman agrees, and I nod.

"Okay, so I need to get her alone, somewhere private, for at least fifteen minutes so that I can explain shifters and fated mates to her. Anything else?"

My friends all share a look, trying to think if they're missing something, and then turn back to me.

"No, I think that's it. You might want to be prepared to shift in front of her," Roman says, and I nod.

"Okay."

"Is your shift over?" Asher asks me, and I nod.

"Yeah, five minutes ago."

"I'll walk you to the lockers. I need to grab something from mine."

"Sounds good. See you guys later," I say to Roman and Jax.

They wave as Asher and I head down the hallway to the locker room. We turn the corner, and Asher clears his throat. I glance over at him and see his brows knitted as he thinks something over.

"What?" I ask him.

"Are you really going to claim your mate?" He whispers as we pass by some nurses.

"I think so. I need to learn more about her. My wolf has been so restless lately, and then after we met her, he became almost unbearable," I tell him as my wolf lunges inside me again.

"How so?" Asher asks.

"He's fighting with me more. He keeps trying to get out. I barely slept last night with him pacing around inside me."

Asher nods as we push the door of the locker room open and head down the row of lockers to ours.

"I just... I need to try to figure out if I can live without my mate or not now that I've found her. I thought I could, that I would be happier on my own and never have to go through losing someone again, but now that I've met Kaia, I'm not so sure."

Asher's jaw is tight, and he is stiff as a board. I know that mates can be a sensitive topic for him, and I try to think of something else to say.

"Good luck," he tells me as he grabs his wallet from his locker and heads back to the ER.

I get showered and changed before I grab my own things and head out to my car. I intended on heading home and coming up with a game plan for what to do with Kaia, but instead, I find myself headed out to the ski lodge on the other side of town.

I park out front, staring up at the hotel side of the resort and debating my next steps.

What's the plan here? Just walk in and ask for her room? She won't be alone. She might not even be in her room.

My wolf growls inside of me, and I sigh. Now that we're here, he's not going to let us leave until we see her again.

I climb out of my car, trying to practice my speech as I head towards the front door.

"Micah?"

I freeze in my tracks at the sound of my name coming in her sweet voice. My wolf is practically salivating as we turn to face Kaia. She's standing a few feet away from me, her wrist still wrapped in the bandage I put on her last night.

She's holding a bag of takeout, and she smiles as she takes a step closer to me.

"Hey," I stammer.

"Hey. What are you doing here?" She asks.

"Um, I was looking for you, actually. I wanted to see how you were doing."

"I'm good. I didn't even need to take any pain medicine this afternoon," she says with a sunny smile.

"That's great. Have you been taking it easy today?" I ask, worry starting to creep in.

"Yeah, we just walked around downtown and did some window shopping," she says.

"You didn't see anything that you liked?" I ask.

"I did, but I couldn't justify getting it."

"What was it?" I ask curiously.

"This antique ring at the Aspen Jewelers. It had this big pink diamond in the center, and it was calling to me, you know? But I don't know where I would ever wear it."

My wolf and I are already imagining her wearing it while we fuck her in our bed, and I clear my throat, trying to focus on our mate.

"Hey, what are you doing tomorrow night?" I ask her.

I need to ask her out before I chicken out. My wolf is tense inside me as we wait to see how this conversation goes. Anxiety swirls inside of me, and I swallow hard.

"Um, I don't know. Why?"

"I was wondering if you would want to go out to dinner with me," I say in a rush, and she blinks.

"Like a date?" She asks, and I nod, not trusting my own voice. "Okay."

"Really?" I blurt out, and she laughs.

"Yeah. What time?"

"Six?" I suggest, and she nods. "I'll pick you up here."

"Alright, I'll see you then."

She gives me one more smile before she turns and heads inside the hotel, the bag of food swinging by her side.

I watch her go until she steps onto the elevator and disappears from view. I know that I need to go home and get some sleep before my shift at the hospital tomorrow morning, but my wolf is fighting me once again.

He wants to stay here. He wants to follow after her and try to talk to her some more.

The mating moon is coming up in a few days, and I know that I'll need to make a decision about claiming Kaia before then.

I can't deny that I want her. She's gorgeous and makes me feel like I'm on top of the world. The choice seems clear when I focus on that, but I can't help but remember losing my parents. I was a shell for so long after I lost them. I was lost, bereft, devastated. Can I handle going through that again if I mark and claim Kaia, and something happens to her?

Why would fate do this to me? Why would they make my mate be someone who is so accident-prone?

I'm not going to get any answers tonight, and I sigh as I head back to my car. It's a struggle for me to climb back into my car, but I manage to calm my wolf and me down by reminding both of us that we'll see her tomorrow.

For our date.

FIVE

Kaia

I THOUGHT I would feel nervous on my first date or any first date, but I feel oddly calm as I sit across the table from Micah. It's like some part of me knows that this is exactly where I'm meant to be.

"So, you've been all over then? That's so cool. What was your favorite place?" He asks me after the waiter leaves to put our orders in.

"Oh, that's a tough one. I liked Pigeon Forge, Tennessee. Kingsley and I went hiking and stayed in this cute little cabin."

"You like being outdoors then?"

"Yeah. I always thought it was weird to go see a new place and spend the whole time at the hotel or spa."

"Same," he says.

He smiles at me, a twinkle in his blue eyes, and my heart flips over in my chest. It's been doing that a lot whenever Micah looks at me. Every time I have his attention on me, it feels like I've been plugged into an outlet.

He looks at me like I'm a princess. He makes me feel beautiful and special, something a man has never made me feel before.

"What about you? Do you like to travel?" I ask him.

"When I have the time. I haven't been to many places, though. Just a few around Alaska."

"Do you like the cold more than the heat?" I ask him.

"I'm not sure that I have a preference. I just like being close to nature."

"I'm the same way," I say with a smile.

The waiter comes back and drops off some bread for us. We both dig in, and I take a bite of bread.

It almost immediately gets lodged in my throat.

I'm not even sure what went wrong. One second, I'm happy and breathing just fine. The next, I'm coughing, trying to dislodge the piece of bread.

"Hold on, I've got you," Micah says, shooting up from his chair and rushing over to my side of the table.

His strong arms wrap around me, and he starts to perform the Heimlich maneuver on me. The piece of bread goes flying out of my mouth, and I suck in a deep breath, coughing as I do.

"Thanks," I wheeze, and he pats me on the back.

"Are you okay?" He asks with concern.

"Yeah, I'm good."

We each take our seats again, and I can feel my face flaming hot with a blush.

"I'm sorry, that's never happened to me before," I start, and Micah smiles at me, though it looks strained and a little fake.

"I'm glad that I was here to help."

I nod, and an awkward silence settles over us. I take a smaller bite of bread and chew it about a million times before I swallow.

Micah clears his throat. I search my brain, trying to figure out what to say to break this terrible silence.

"What about your family?" I blurt out. "Are they in Aspen Ridge too?"

"No, they passed away when I was a kid."

I should have just kept my mouth shut.

"Oh, Micah, I'm so sorry," I say sincerely, and he nods.

"Thanks. It was a long time ago."

"It still must have been hard."

He nods, and it's pretty obvious that he doesn't want to have this conversation.

"What made you choose to go into medicine?" I try.

"I've always been interested in helping people. I wanted to be useful to my p... community," he says, clearing his throat, and I smile.

"That sounds noble of you."

"Maybe. The paycheck doesn't hurt either," he admits, and I smile.

"I'm sure."

"What about you? How's the social media company?"

"It's going well. We started it when we were juniors in college, and it's grown from there. We didn't have as much time this year to focus on growing it, but now that we've graduated, we're hoping to invest more time and energy into making it a success."

"I'm sure you will," he says, and I smile.

"We have two months to try. Then we'll have to seriously look at getting different jobs," I tell him.

The waiter comes by with our food, and I moan at the sight of my spaghetti covered in parmesan cheese.

"Is this your favorite restaurant in town?" I ask as we both dig in.

"There aren't many options, but this place is always good. It's really one of the only good date places in town," he says, and I smile.

"Well, I like it."

The little Italian restaurant is right on the main street, tucked between a charming little bookstore and a pet store. The place is dimly lit, with twinkling candles on every table. It gives it a romantic vibe that I fell in love with as soon as I walked in.

I take another bite and reach for my water glass. When I set my glass back down, my elbow hits the side of my plate, and I gasp as marinara sauce, spaghetti, and meatballs slides off the plate and directly into my lap.

Maybe I should just give up now. This date keeps hitting bumps in the road. I'm not sure that I can stand any more embarrassment tonight.

"I can't believe I just did that," I groan, covering my face in my hands.

"It's fine. I'll get you another order," he says as he comes to help me clean up the mess.

"I'm just going to run to the bathroom and try to wipe some of this off," I tell him as I stand and head toward the bathroom.

I manage to trip twice on my way there, and I debate just staying in here for the rest of the night.

My phone buzzes in my back pocket, and I pull it out, smiling when I see that it's a message from Kingsley.

KINGSLEY: How's the date going?

Kaia: I've tripped at least three times, spilled pasta all

over myself, and managed to choke on a bite of bread. So great.

Kingsley: I bet he proposes to you before the night is over.

Kaia: LOL!

Kaia: Doubt it. I'm sure that I'll be home soon. He's probably looking for a reason to cut this date short by now.

Kingsley: Bring me some garlic bread!

Kaia: The one that I choked on?

Kingsley: LOL! Preferably not.

Kaia: I'll try.

I TUCK my phone back into my jeans and do my best to wipe off the marinara and spaghetti. I wore my nicest jeans tonight since I didn't have anything fancier. Now I'm kind of upset since I'm sure they're ruined now.

I sigh, staring at my reflection in the mirror. My blonde hair has a few splatters of marinara sauce in it, but other than that, looks shiny and pretty, hanging in soft waves around my shoulders.

My black knit sweater was meant to make me look slimmer, but now that it's half covered in spaghetti sauce, I'm not sure I'm pulling it off.

I knew going into tonight that this would just be a vacation fling. It was meant to be a way for me to dip my toe into the dating pool and gain some experience. Instead, all it's taught me is that I'm probably going to die alone.

I take a deep breath, square my shoulders, and head to the door.

I promptly run smack into Micah.

"Sorry," he says, catching me by my shoulders before I

can fall. "I didn't see you there. I was coming to check on you. Are you okay?"

"I'm good. I should have been looking where I was going," I apologize.

"I had the waiter bag up our food. I thought you might want to go back to the hotel and shower instead of sitting in spaghetti," he says with a kind smile.

This must be his way of ending the date gently.

I force myself to smile and let him lead me out of the restaurant. He gets the passenger door for me before he sets the plastic bag of our food in the backseat and heads around to the driver's side.

He smiles at me as he starts the car, and I force myself to smile back.

"Sorry about tonight. This was my first date, and I think maybe I need a bit more practice at things like walking and eating before I try again," I joke.

He laughs at that, seeming to relax, and I sink further into my seat.

"It's no big deal. I actually had a lot of fun. It was cool to hear about your travels and Kingsley. I'm glad that you have such a close friend."

"She's basically my sister," I agree.

"I wish I had that."

"I thought that you had friends here in town?"

He had told me about his fellow doctors and friends at the hospital earlier when I had told him what Kingsley and I had been up to today.

Things start to relax between the two of us once again. It's hard to keep up with the shift between us. It's like neither of us is sure that we really want to dive all into this relationship or not.

That's probably for the best anyway, considering that

Kingsley and I leave in three days. I can't be falling head over heels for someone that lives here when I'll be heading to Hawaii in a few days and then back home after that.

Still, I can't deny that my attraction to Micah is still there. I've never felt this way about anyone before, and it's hard to ignore how much I want him.

Micah pulls up in front of the hotel and hops out to get my door for me.

"Thanks," I say.

The temperature is starting to drop now that the sun has set and I shiver as the wind whips my hair around my face.

"I had fun tonight," he says, stepping closer to me and blocking out the wind.

"Me too," I say, and I'm surprised to admit that I actually did.

Sure, there were a few hiccups, but overall, I like being around Micah. He makes me feel at peace and cared for.

"Maybe we could do this again. Tomorrow night?" He asks, and I blink.

"Sure," I say with a wide smile. "I'd like that."

"How about I cook for you?"

"Sounds good."

We smile at each other, and I find myself swaying towards him slightly. Maybe it was the wind or maybe there's just something about Micah that draws me in. Either way, our lips are now a breath away from each other, and I lick my lips, drawing his eyes there.

"Kaia," he breathes, and my nipples harden in my bra.

"Please," I beg, and he closes the gap between us.

He cups my face in his hands, and I love the feeling of his hands on my skin. He cradles my face so carefully, like

I'm something precious, and my heart starts to race in my chest.

His lips are soft underneath mine, and they mold to mine perfectly. It's like we're meant to be. Like we were made for each other.

His tongue slides against the seam of my lips, and I open for him tentatively. This is all so new to me, and I wonder if he can tell that I've never been kissed before.

He slips his tongue inside my mouth, and I cling to his thick biceps as I start to lose myself in his kiss and touch. It feels like if I don't hold onto something, then I'll be swept away in the current.

My tongue brushes against his, and we both moan. One of his hands wraps around the back of my neck, and he pulls me tighter against him. I like this dominant side of him. I want him to show me how to kiss and make love. I want to feel his hands all over my body.

He pulls back, and I lick my lips, desperate for another taste of him. His lips are swollen and red and wet. I can't help but wonder if mine look the same way.

I look up and see the desperate heat filling his blue eyes, and it makes me want to throw myself at him all over again.

"I'll text you," he says, and I smile as he passes me the bag of food.

"Okay," I say, taking the food and turning to head into the hotel.

I can't help but glance over my shoulder as I head inside, and I smile when I see that he's staring after me too.

I head up to the room, and Kingsley opens the door for me before I can try to dig out my key.

"Hey, how was it?" She asks, noticing my smile.

"Really good, actually," I say, my lips still tingling from his kiss.

"I see that you brought food."

"Yeah, Micah ordered more after I dumped mine all over me."

"Aww," she says, and I smile as she starts to dig through the bag.

She pulls out five take-out boxes, and I wonder what all he ordered. She starts to open the boxes, and my mouth drops when I see that he ordered two of the spaghetti and meatballs, along with three desserts.

"There's a note," Kingsley says, and I grab it from her.

I DIDN'T WANT **you and Kingsley to go hungry. Let me know which one is your favorite.**

X.

Micah

MY HEART AND STOMACH FLIP, and I grin to myself as Kingsley passes me a fork.

"Dig in."

SIX

Micah

I KNOW before my second date with Kaia is even over that I'll never be able to resist her. With every passing minute, I fall even more in love with her. She's just so perfect for me, and it's hard to resist that.

My wolf doesn't know why we ever even bothered. He was never going to let her leave without claiming her. He's been pacing inside me and counting down the seconds until we can bite her and make her ours forever.

I don't know why we ever even tried to resist her. I mean, she's fated to be ours. We never stood a chance. Besides, I'm a doctor, and once I mark her, she'll get some of my properties. That should help make her a little less breakable and vulnerable. If she does get hurt, then I can help heal her. It's like my calling to become a doctor was all leading to this.

"That smells so good," Kaia says as she swivels back and forth in her barstool.

"It's almost done," I say, stirring the simmering pasta sauce on the stove.

We're at my house tonight. I wanted to be somewhere a little more private so that I can tell Kaia about shifters and fated mates. I've been going over everything the guys told me the other day about having this conversation, and I'm prepared to answer all of her questions and even shift for her.

I already gave her a tour of my place. She seemed to like my cabin, and I'm glad. I fell in love with this place when I saw it, and I was worried that she might want something a little more modern or upscale. I've always liked the more rustic look, and it seems like Kaia might feel the same way.

She will. We're perfect for each other, my wolf reminds me, and I smile.

I've made us dinner, chicken alfredo, the only thing that I know how to cook well, and the plan is to bring up shifters and me being a wolf one over dinner. I'm nervous about how she'll take it, but I know that we need to have this conversation before the mating moon tomorrow night.

Now that I've decided to mark her and make her mine, it's like a weight has been lifted off of my shoulders. I'm going to tell her that we're meant to be tonight, and then tomorrow, I'm going to make her mine.

Ours, my wolf growls, and I smile.

"Ours," I correct myself.

"What's that?" Kaia asks, and I clear my throat.

"I said I hope you're hungry," I lie, and she smiles.

"Starving. Are you sure that you don't need help with anything?"

"I've got it," I say, turning off the burner and grabbing the plates from the counter.

The garlic bread is cooling on the stove, and I slice up

the chicken, adding a healthy serving of spaghetti noodles, alfredo, and chicken to each plate. Kaia grins at me as I set a plate down in front of her and then take my seat next to her.

"This looks amazing. I didn't think you could cook," she says as we dig in.

"This is pretty much all that I can make," I admit, and she smiles.

"Well, you make it well," she says, taking another bite.

"Thanks. What did you and Kingsley do today?" I ask her.

"We tried out the slopes."

"And no injuries?" I ask her.

She laughs, shaking her head, and my stomach sinks.

"Not quite. We did the bunny slopes, but I still managed to fall down quite a few times. I'm pretty sure I have at least one bruise on my legs, arms, and butt."

She laughs, and I try to join her, but the thought of her hurt still makes me feel uneasy.

Bite her now, my wolf urges me, and I grit my teeth, holding him back. *We need to tell her about shifters and fated mates first;* I remind him. He sighs, rolls his eyes, and starts to pace inside me.

"Well, I'm glad that nothing was broken, at least," I say, and she smiles.

"Me too. I need to be able to walk around for the rest of our vacation," she says.

"You've been this clumsy since you were a kid, right?" I ask her, and she nods.

"What about you? What were you like as a kid?"

My brain throws up a wall at the idea of remembering a time that was so painful, but I would give my mate anything.

My wolf paces inside me, restless, as I take a drink of water and clear my throat.

"I was pretty lonely. After my parents died, I was pretty much just on my own. I didn't have any other family."

"I'm so sorry. I can't even imagine," she says softly, and I swallow hard.

"It was...rough," I admit. "But I got through it."

"I wish that hadn't happened to you. I'm so sorry, Micah," she says.

Her green eyes are filled with compassion, and my wolf brushes against me. He wants to move closer to her, to have her scent covering us. I force him down and smile at her.

"Do you have a big family?"

"Kind of. I'm an only child, but so is Kingsley. Our parents are super close, and she's always felt like my sister. We went on a lot of vacations and stuff together."

"That must have been nice."

"It was. We're all still close. They're on a vacation together right now in Thailand while Kingsley and I are up here."

"Sounds fun."

She smiles widely at me, and we share a moment. I can feel our connection growing, becoming stronger, and my wolf wags his tail in excitement. I smile back at her, and she glances away, down to her plate. We both dig into our food, and it's silent for a few moments.

"What do you do for fun?" I ask.

"I like reading, watching movies or tv, hanging out with friends. Kingsley and I love to travel. We've been all over the US. Well, except for Hawaii, but that's where we're headed next."

"What will you do after you've been everywhere?" I ask her, and she grins.

"Head to Europe!"

I laugh, and she joins in.

"What about you? What do you like to do for fun?"

"It's been so long since I've had any fun," I try to joke, but it's kind of true. "I love to read and play sports with my friends. Usually, I'm busy at the hospital, though."

She nods, and my wolf growls at me. He wants me to tell her about shifters and fated mates already. I know that things with my wolf are going to get more tense if I don't get this over with, so I clear my throat, gathering my thoughts.

"I wanted to talk to you about something," I say, breaking the silence, and she glances up at me.

"About what?" She asks innocently, and I take a deep breath.

"Have you ever heard of shifters or fated mates?" I ask her.

"Um, what?"

I'll take that as a no then...

"It's like werewolves. Someone who can switch and change back and forth between a human and an animal."

"Okay," she says, staring at me blankly.

"There's a ton of different animals, though, not just wolves. A shifter can be any type of animal."

"Uh-huh," she says, still watching me with that blank look on her face.

I wish that I could read it, but I power through. Everything between us is so easy and natural, and I know she can feel it too.

"I'm a wolf shifter. A lot of people who live in this section of Aspen Ridge are."

"Okay."

"Shifters also have fated mates."

I've switched to doctor mode now. I'm talking analytically and am just focused on the facts, but this fated mate part might require a bit more emotion.

"A fated mate is someone that you're literally fated to be with. You're mine. That means you're the only one I will ever love or want. That we're meant to be. Shifters can really only claim their mates on a full moon. We call it the mating moon because this heat will hit us, and we'll be insatiable for each other."

"Right," she says, shifting in her barstool.

She's stopped eating, and I wonder if she's full already. Maybe now would be a good time to shift for her.

"My wolf would like to meet you," I say, standing from my stool and reaching for the hem of my shirt.

I don't wait for her response as I strip out of my clothes and then shift before she can say anything. I land on my four paws, and my wolf steps toward Kaia, nudging at her hand.

He's so happy to finally meet her and smell her sweet scent in our home. He wants to bring her upstairs and have her lay in our bed so we can fall asleep with her scent surrounding us.

Kaia leaps to her feet and stumbles back a few steps, and I blink, wondering what's going on. She's breathing fast and staring at me with wide eyes. I can recognize it then. She's overwhelmed. I put too much on her too fast.

"I need to go," she rushes to say, and before I can shift back, she's turning and rushing to the front door.

I shift as the door slams shut behind her, and that's when it hits me.

I've been so wrapped up in trying to decide if I wanted to claim her or not that I never really even considered the possibility of her rejecting me.

My wolf whines inside me, curling up into a ball, and I slump into my chair as I stare at the closed front door.

What am I supposed to do now?

SEVEN

Kaia

"AND THEN HE JUST... turned into a wolf," Kingsley asks for the tenth time in the last hour.

I nod, collapsing back against the mattress and covering my face with my hands. I groan and feel the bed dip next to me as Kingsley takes a seat next to me.

"And you weren't drunk or anything?" She asks.

I crack my fingers and glare up at her.

"No, I was stone-cold sober. How many more times are we going to go over all of this?"

"I just... I don't know. None of this is making sense."

"Tell me about it," I grumble.

I sigh as I sit up and scrub my hands down my face again.

"And you're meant to be with him?" She asks, and I nod.

"That's what he said. That we were fated mates. We were meant to be, and he would only ever want me."

"And do you believe him?" She asks me, and I pause.

That's the part that I keep getting hung up on. I keep replaying everything that happened last night over and over in my head, but I can't seem to come up with an answer on what to do next.

I really liked Micah. When he first started talking about shifters and fated mates, I was caught off guard. When he told me that he was a wolf shifter, I was worried that he was having some kind of mental break or that maybe he was crazy and my guy radar was just way off.

Then he shifted in front of me, and I realized he was telling the truth. And I didn't know what to do with that.

If he was telling the truth about being a wolf shifter, then was he telling the truth about the mating heat and us being meant to be? Part of me hopes that he's right. I've never felt this way before about anyone, and maybe he's right about us being fated to be together. That would explain why he's the only man I've ever been attracted to.

Still, I've only known him for a few days. What am I supposed to do with any of this information anyway? Can I move here? I know I can do my job from anywhere with the internet, but it's going against my plans with Kingsley. My plans for myself. Can I give up all of that? Give up being close to my family, all for a guy I just met?

A shiver runs through me. I've been feeling different ever since I woke up this morning. I can't quite explain it. There's this feeling of awareness like all my senses are cranked up to eleven.

I can't stop thinking about him, can't stop thinking about what it would feel like to have his body on mine, pressing me down into the mattress or whatever surface we're up against.

Heat blossoms inside me, threatening to overheat me, and I clear my throat, trying to clear my head.

I wonder if this is the mating heat that he was talking about. It is the full moon tonight...

"I need to get out of here and clear my head," I tell Kingsley, and she nods.

"Let's try skiing again. We were getting pretty good yesterday," she suggests, and I nod.

"Let's go."

We both grab our winter gear and start getting bundled up. The ski resort part is just a short distance from the hotel, so it takes us no time to get there. We rent some skis and get in line for the ski lift. If I'm honest, I think that the ski lift is my favorite part of this whole skiing business.

"Stay on the bunny slope, right?" Kingsley asks when we come up to the first drop.

"Yeah, I'm not sure I'm ready for any of the bigger hills yet," I say, and she laughs.

"Me either. I think that I fell more times than you did yesterday."

I laugh, but it's weak. I'm still thinking about Micah and what I should do next.

We hop off the ski lift and make our way over the top of the bunny hill. The hill is dotted with little kids and their parents, and I wait for the little girl in front of me to go before I ski up to the edge of the hill.

"Ready?" Kingsley asks, and I nod distractedly.

I need to stop thinking about Micah and focus on skiing and hanging out with Kingsley.

We use our poles and push off.

It starts so well.

Then I start to wobble.

The next thing that I know, I'm falling face-first into the snow.

I try to brace my fall, but I'm going too fast. Pain shoots up my arm, and I know that it's at least sprained before I even come to a stop. I've lost one of my skis halfway up the small hill and look up to see Kingsley running up the hill toward me; concern etched into her features.

"Are you okay?" She asks breathlessly, and I shake my head.

"My arm," I say, and she nods, not needing me to go on.

"Let's get you to the hospital."

I stand, and she gathers up our skis and poles. She drops them off at the rental hut and then runs ahead to get the car. By the time I walk up to the front, she's waiting for me.

"Think he'll be there?" She asks as we drive toward the hospital.

"Probably," I grumble, clutching my wrist.

It's the opposite wrist that I hurt the night I first met Micah, and I hold it tight to my chest as we head down Main Street.

I can't deny that part of me is excited at the prospect that I might see Micah again. Anticipation and a warm blush start to encompass me, and I squirm in my seat.

Kingsley pulls into a parking spot in front of the hospital, and we both hop out.

"I'll get your wallet," she says when I start to reach for it.

"Thanks."

We walk in and don't even get to the front reception desk before Micah is onto me.

"Mat—Kaia," he corrects, and I feel a blush stain my cheeks.

"Hi," I say, almost shyly.

Now that he's in front of me, all those feelings seem to get more intense. I want to touch him. I want to feel his skin against mine. I want him to bite me.

Wait, what?

"What's wrong?" He asks, panic filling his eyes as he looks down at my wrist.

There's a different kind of energy surrounding Micah today too. He's almost... feral as he looks me over. His blue eyes look like they're glowing as he stares at me, and I can see a muscle in his jaw pop as he grinds his teeth together.

"I fell skiing. I think it might be sprained."

"Let's check it out," he says, putting his hand on the small of my back and leading me down the hallway.

I try to pretend that his touch isn't sending tingles throughout my whole body, but I'm not sure I'm pulling it off. My nipples are aching buds inside my bra, and they're so sensitive from rubbing against the fabric with each step or breath, and I have the strongest urge to moan.

The lower the sun sinks in the sky, the hornier I seem to become. My panties are drenched now, and I desperately want to change them, but I'm sure I would just soak through the next pair too.

I can feel the mating pull that Micah was talking about last night. I guess I didn't take him seriously or maybe I just didn't realize that the pull would be this strong. I have the urge to brush my body against him, but there are people around.

I'm a virgin, but it wasn't like I was saving myself for someone. I just never met anyone I wanted to sleep with, but I definitely want to sleep with Micah. I've been thinking about this all day. I want him, but is this connection between us real, or is it just nature pushing us together? After the full moon, will I regret giving myself to him? I can't deny that my body wants him. Is this a fling? Or something more?

I was attracted to Micah even before this whole mating moon thing, but this feels like more. It feels like this connection, this lust, is a living, breathing thing in the room with us.

I want to give in to him and this connection between us more than anything, but if I do, then what happens next? Is the attraction or chase going to be over for him?

I sigh, trying to clear my head, but it's no use. It's hard to think straight with my hormones raging out of control.

Micah leads me into an exam room, and I glance back, noticing Kingsley taking a seat in the lobby. I wonder if she can feel this thing between us, too, and is trying to give us space.

The door closes, and I turn to look at Micah. Now that we're alone, all I can think about is Micah stripping me naked and bending me over this exam room table.

"How, uh, how did you hurt it?" He asks me.

He seems different today. At first, I thought it was because of how I left yesterday, but now I'm thinking it's something else.

He's barely looking at me, and when he does, he looks almost angry. He's tense and clearly on edge. A muscle in his jaw keeps popping, and I wonder why he looks like he's holding himself back from something.

"We were skiing, and I just fell and landed on it wrong. I don't think that it's broken," I tell him.

Why does my voice sound like that? So husky and wanton.

I clear my throat and hope it helps me not sound like I'm dying for him to fuck me.

I watch as Micah moves around the exam room, taking in the tense set of his shoulders as he washes his hands. I know how I feel right now and wonder if it's the same for him.

Could that be why he's acting so strange?

I look down to see the bulge in his jeans.

I guess so...

The ache builds stronger in my core, and a breathy moan escapes my lips as Micah bends over to throw his paper towel away.

Maybe if I can just go back to the hotel, I can rub one out, and this feeling will pass. I just need to make it through this exam.

Micah turns back to me, his face set in determined lines, and I can't stay in this room any longer.

"Maybe I should go?"

"No," he says, his tone firm.

He grits his teeth, his jaw ticking beneath his skin as he moves toward me.

"I need to check you out – check out your wrist," he corrects.

"O-o-okay," I stammer.

The pull only grows stronger as he gets closer to me, and I bite my bottom lip so hard that I can almost taste blood.

His fingers move over my arm gently, and it's practically foreplay. His touch is so light, just a whisper against my skin, and I can't stop the moan this time.

We both stiffen at the sound, and I see him swallow hard. His eyes roam over me, and I press my thighs together tighter.

I'm seconds away from begging him to take me when he steps back, his hands curling into fists.

"Did you hurt anything else?" He asks; his tone so low and filled with filthy promises. "Any other aches or pains?"

"Uh-huh," I say before I can think better of it.

The ache that I'm talking about is between my legs, and it's only growing stronger with each passing second. I have a feeling that Micah is the only one who can make it better.

"I'll need to check over all of you then and make sure there's nothing else injured. Then we can get X-rays on your wrist."

I nod, not trusting myself to speak right now.

"Can you stand up, please?" He asks, and I hurry to slip off of the exam table.

"You can put this on," he says, passing me a hospital gown.

He turns around, giving me his back, and I reach for my clothes with shaky hands. Having him just feet away while I strip is so erotic. Goosebumps spread across my skin and I take a deep breath.

I push my pants down, and they pool at my feet. It's then that I start to feel self-conscious. I'm by no means a small girl, and I wonder if Micah is going to have second thoughts when he sees me naked.

I don't need to worry, though.

"Ready?" Micah asks, turning around.

He lets out a guttural groan when he sees me standing before him, naked. My nipples ache, and my pussy clamps down around nothing. I'm so empty and achy. I need him.

"Micah," I sob, and he's on me.

His hands cup the back of my head, tangle in my hair, and tug so that he can claim my mouth with his.

"I've got you. I'll make it better," he promises me, and I nod.

"I need you," I admit.

"Thank fuck. God, you're so fucking beautiful. Better than a fucking dream," he whispers against my lips, and I blush, pressing my curves closer to his body.

His lips mold to mine, and I moan in my throat. I want to climb him, already I'm anxious to have him between my legs, but first, we need him to lose his clothes.

"Your turn," I whisper when he finally lets me come up for air.

He looks uncertain for a moment, and I wonder if he's really worried about getting naked in front of me.

"Are you sure about this?" He asks me, and my heart softens at the concern in his eyes.

"I'm sure."

My wrist is just a dull throb now. The ache between my legs is my greater focus, and I help him take off his clothes. My jaw drops as I take in all of his muscles and tanned skin.

"So handsome," I say, and he grins down at me.

That's all it takes to have him taking control again.

He kisses me, and I cling to him. His body is so hard, so hot against mine, and it has me feeling like I'm about to burn up.

I'm way past feeling insecure. As long as he keeps kissing and touching me, I'm happy. His hands cup my breasts, molding the soft globes in his hands, and we both moan.

"Micah, I need you. Please, please, you have to take the ache away," I plead.

His lips slam down on mine, and I let him devour me as he pushes me back toward the exam table. His tongue presses against the seam of me, and I open for him, just as greedy for him as he is for me.

I hit the edge of the table, and Micah pushes me back.

"Lay down, mate. I'm going to take care of you."

I'm panting in need, and I hurry to do as he orders. I always thought I would want my first time to be slow and gentle, but now that it's actually happening, I just want Micah to take me hard. I need to come so damn bad.

"Please," I moan, and he nods, kissing his way down my body.

His lips linger at the base of my neck, and I tense, waiting for him to do...something. There's a sense of anticipation, but I don't understand it.

He kisses lower, across my clavicle, and I sigh.

"That feels so good," I breathe as he kisses his way down my chest.

"So perfect," he says back.

He maneuvers me over to the edge of the exam table and comes down over me. I spread my legs, aching to feel him inside me, but he avoids any contact and focuses on my breasts.

His head drops, and I watch the top of his dark head as he licks a circle around my areola.

"Oh god," I gasp, and he growls.

"You only say my name," he orders, and I nod.

"Micah. Please," I beg, and he grins but gives me what I need.

His lips wrap around one stiff peak, and he sucks it into his mouth. The action has me bowing off the exam table, desperate for him to give me more.

"So responsive," he praises me, and I blush, widening my legs. "And so greedy," he teases.

I whine, the sound high-pitched as I throw my head back against the exam table. The paper covering it crinkles as my hands grip it.

"Don't worry, Kaia. I'm going to give you what you need."

His hand drifts over my stomach as he goes back to teasing my nipples. He grips my restless hips, pinning me in place, and I cry out.

"Gorgeous," he says, giving my nipple one last lick before he starts to kiss his way down my body.

He spreads my thighs wide, his fingers trailing up my thighs, and I hold my breath as he dips his thumb into my dripping core. I'm soaked, and his finger easily slides through my folds.

"Yes," I groan.

That quickly turns into a whine when he pulls back.

"I need a taste," he growls, and I nod.

I think that I would agree to anything right now as long as he didn't stop touching me like this.

Micah drops to his knees at the edge of the exam table before I can blink, and I gasp as he grabs my thighs, spreading them wide before he buries his face in my wet pussy.

He doesn't waste any time, and I know then that he's just as on edge as I am. I cry out as his tongue rolls over my clit, and my hands go to his hair, tangling in the strands and trying to hold him there. I don't think that there's any need. He doesn't seem to have any intention of moving from between my legs.

He licks up my core, dipping his tongue inside me and then moving up to circle my little button. He repeats the same path over and over again, and it doesn't take me long before I'm right on the edge again.

When Micah pushes one thick digit inside of me, I come so hard that I see stars, but he doesn't stop. He fucks me with his finger, stretching me as he continues to lick my clit over and over again.

He prolongs my orgasm, and I barely come down when he sends me flying over the edge once again.

"Oh my gosh, Micah," I moan as he kisses the inside of my thigh.

He grins against my skin, and I sit up, resting on my elbows to look down at him.

"Is it my turn now?" I ask, my cheeks heating as I think about sucking his cock.

"I need between these pretty thighs."

I shake my head, wanting to please him as much as he just did me. I'm desperate for it.

As soon as he stands, I'm off the table and kneeling at his feet. His dick is pointing straight at me, and I feel myself get wetter as I wrap my fingers around it.

He's bigger than I expected and thick. My fingers don't even touch, and I wonder how I'm going to get him in my mouth, let alone my pussy.

"Kaia," he starts, but I don't want him to try to talk me out of it, so I lean in, opening my mouth as wide as I can over the tip of him.

"Fuck," he hisses out between his teeth, and I smile, licking a path up the underside of his cock and tracing the vein there.

My hand wraps around the base of him. I should probably be feeling some kind of pain as I grip him, but all I can feel is the mating heat. It's taken over all of my senses and I hum as I take him in my mouth again, setting up a rhythm with both as I start to suck.

He tastes like man and earth, and I moan at his flavor. His fingers tangle in my hair, and I look up at him, my green eyes meeting his blue ones.

He looks like he's right on the brink, and I suck him harder.

"That's enough! I need you," he growls, reaching down and pulling me up.

He pushes me back down onto the exam table, and I grin up at him as he reaches down, roughly jerking my legs apart.

"I have to bite you," he tells me, and I nod at him.

"Yes. Bite me. Please," I beg, twisting my head to the side.

I don't even understand what is happening, but it feels so right.

He brackets my body with his strong arms and leans down. I feel his warm breath on my skin a second before his teeth sink into the sensitive flesh.

I cry out, moaning as pleasure courses through me, and he takes the opportunity to sink into me. I scream again as he breaks through my virginity, but it's not in pain. It's in pleasure.

I come as soon as he's fully seated inside me, and Micah growls. He doesn't give me time to adjust before he's drawing his hips back and slamming into me.

He fucks me hard, and I can feel myself tightening around him. Sweat coats my skin, and when he licks over the bite mark, sealing the wound, I feel another orgasm slam into me.

"MICAH!" I scream, and he does it again.

It's so sensitive, and every time he brushes over it, I come. I've lost track of how many orgasms I've had. I'm powerless to do anything but let Micah claim me.

He grips one of my thighs, hoisting it higher on his hip as he ruts into me. This changes the angle, and he hits my clit now with each stroke.

"Oh god," I sob, and I see him grit his teeth.

My pussy starts to spasm around his length, and I groan

as another wave slams into me. This time I take Micah with me, and I moan as I feel his hot release splash against my walls.

I suck in a deep breath and stare up at Micah. He's breathing just as hard, a thin layer of sweat covering his forehead.

"I need more," I tell him, lust still swirling inside me.

"Not here. I'm taking you home," he says.

He grabs my hand, and I notice that my wrist is no longer sore. He must see me frowning at it because he smiles.

"You have some of my shifter properties now. One of them being advanced healing. It's all better now."

"Whoa," I breathe, and he grins.

"Get dressed. I have plans for you, mate."

"What about your shift?"

"It ended five minutes ago," he tells me and my heart starts to race with the promise in his eyes.

"Kinsley is waiting for me."

"I'll send her back to the hotel."

Hearing him growl at me like that has me so turned on, and I hurry to do what he ordered.

My whole body feels well-used, and I smile as I tug on my shoes. I have a feeling that it's going to be a long night. A long and amazing night.

EIGHT

Micah

I WAKE up wrapped around my mate. Kaia's hair is fanned across my chest and face, and I smile as I breathe in her sweet scent. My cock is still buried between her legs. I had made love to her so many times last night, and at some point, we both must have passed out. Now that we're awake, I'm ready to start all over again.

I can still remember how it felt to want my mate yesterday. The need to bite her and claim her only grew with each passing second, and when she had come in for her wrist, I had barely been able to hold myself back.

I knew I would feel the mating heat, but I never thought it would be so strong. I had a hard time controlling myself when she wasn't near me. Put her in the same small room as me and my wolf and I could barely hold myself back.

Luckily for me, Kaia could feel it too. I still remember how it felt to see that her nipples were pebbled for me. She could barely sit still and seeing her squirm on the exam table, her curvy thighs pressing together. I loved knowing that she wanted me just as much as I wanted her.

Knowing that she could feel the attraction, too, made me feel better, but it also made holding myself and my wolf back even harder.

I couldn't stop picturing fucking her as I checked out her wrist. As my fingers stroked over her soft skin, all I could imagine was how she would feel under me, her hot little body welcoming my thrusts as I pounded into her.

As I checked out her wrist and got ready to do an X-ray, all I could think about was what it would feel like to have her ride me. I wanted to see her tits bouncing and jiggling as she took all of me. I wanted to feel her cream all over my cock before I flipped her onto her hands and knees and plowed into her from behind.

I made sure to make each of those fantasies come true last night, and I smirk to myself as I replay it in my head.

I can't believe that I ever had doubts about making her mine. I know I was scared of losing her, but now that she's mine, I can't imagine my life without her.

My wolf is curled up inside of me. I can't tell if he's tired from all the activities last night or if maybe he's just content to sleep now that we've made Kaia our mate.

Kaia starts to stir on top of me, and my cock twitches inside her. She moans at the action, and my wolf starts to wake up at the sound.

I know that she must be sore, but when her pussy clamps down around me, I know that she needs me right now just as much as I need her.

"Morning, mate," I whisper as I thrust into her, and she moans louder.

"Morning," she says, rocking her hips down as I thrust up.

"Fuck, Kaia," I groan. "You wouldn't believe that I popped that cherry just last night with how horny you are for it."

She moans louder and tips her hips up, starting to rock against me harder. She's so desperate to fuck me again, and my wolf and I love it. It's a good thing, too, since I'm just as greedy for her.

KAIA SITS up and braces her hands against my chest, rocking her hips as she starts getting lost in her release. I let her bounce on me, using my cock to pleasure herself, and my wolf licks his lips.

Her scent is all around us, and I reach up, tangling my fingers in her pale hair.

"So fucking hot," I moan, and she tips her head back, thrusting her tits into my face.

"I need more," she moans, and I grip her hips, helping her find her rhythm.

"Whatever you need, mate. It's yours."

She bounces on my cock harder, throwing her head back until I can feel her silky hair tickling against the top of my thighs. My hands cup her tits, rolling the pebbled nipples between my fingers as she rides me. I lean up, taking one of the tips into my mouth and rolling it over my tongue. I bite down gently and am rewarded when she tightens around my cock.

"Micah, I need more," she pants, and I release her nipple.

"What do you need, mate? Tell me, and it's yours."

"Touch the mark," she begs, and I lean forward at once,

running my lips over the bite mark that I put on her just last night.

She goes off, and her pussy clamps down so tight around my length that I know it's only a matter of time before I come.

"Don't stop," she pleads, and I roll us again.

I pull out, and she whines, looking at me over her shoulder as I flip her onto her stomach and pull her up onto her hands and knees. I sink back inside her soaked pussy, gripping her wide hips as I pound into her. She moans, turning her head, and our eyes meet. She watches me as I mount her and claim her, and I swear it feels like our souls are joining as she finally reaches her peak.

Her sweet cunt is too good to resist, and I come with her. Hard.

"Fuck, Kaia," I groan, and she sucks in a deep breath.

"Uh-huh," she agrees, and I smile as we both fall back to the mattress.

I spoon behind her, both of us trying to catch our breath. My wolf is sated and happy inside of me, and I smile as I imagine our future now that we have our mate.

"We could wake up like this every day once you move here," I tell her, and she tenses against me.

My wolf whines inside of me when she pulls away from me slightly.

"Kaia?" I ask when she avoids my eyes.

"I... I'm not sure that I'm going to move here," she admits, and now it's my turn to tense.

"You don't like it here?" I ask.

My wolf leaps to his feet inside me and starts to pace in agitation. How did we go from being on top of the world and claiming our mate to about to lose her.

"It's nice… it's just not what I had planned," she says quietly.

Her phone starts to ring, and she rolls away from me. I watch her go, and I can't help but wonder if I'm about to lose her.

Either way, I'm going to have to make a choice.

Do I give up my pack or my mate?

NINE

Kaia

"SO, he asked you to move in then?" Kingsley asks me, and I gulp down half of my coffee before I answer her.

I barely got any sleep last night, and I need all of the caffeine that I can get right now so that I can have this conversation.

I set my cup down, twisting my blonde hair up into a messy bun. It's still tangled and messy from Micah running his fingers through it last night and again this morning. I can't seem to bring myself to take a shower yet, though. I don't want to wash his scent off of me yet.

I just got back to the hotel, and I've been catching her up on everything that happened last night. She had high-fived me when I told her how good the sex was, but her smile had dropped off when I mentioned him talking about me moving him here.

"Kind of. He just started talking like it was a done deal

that I was going to move here and be with him. We never actually talked about it before now, though."

"Do you want to move here?" She asks, and I sigh.

"I don't know. The town has kind of grown on me these last couple of days. I don't want to be away from you, though. I know that I could travel and see you and our parents or still take our trips every few months, but it won't be the same," I tell her.

"What if I moved up here with you?"

"You would do that?" I ask her, and she smiles.

"Sure. I kind of love the town too. I could be happy anywhere, though, as long as I have my best friend," she says with a smile.

She hits her shoulder against mine, and I smile, resting my head on her shoulder.

"Is it too much too fast, though? Part of me feels like I'm giving up so much to be with him, and he's giving up nothing."

"Well, how do you feel about him?" She asks after a minute.

"I love him," I admit quietly. "That whole fated mate thing really was true. I guess I thought soulmates or whatever would be easy, but this has been kind of messy."

"I think that you need to talk to him. Explain all of this and see where he's at. Then you can make an informed decision."

There's my best friend. Kingsley has always been more clear-headed and wise. I don't know what I would do without her.

"I know that you're right and that I need to make a decision before we make any big moves. I think if I tried to live here, I would just fall more in love with him, and then it would be impossible for me to leave. I want to make sure that we really are happy here."

"Talk to your man," she encourages me, and I nod, knowing she's right.

"And if I decide to stay?" I ask.

"Then we stay," she says, wrapping her arm around my shoulders.

"I love you, Kingsley. I couldn't do any of this without you."

"You could. You're so much stronger than you realize."

I smile, blinking back tears as we hug on the bed. My phone starts to ring, and I know without looking that it's Micah.

"You should get that. I'll give you some privacy," she says, and I nod.

I answer the call on the last ring and clear my throat.

"Hello?"

"Kaia," Micah says, sounding relieved. "We need to talk."

"I know," I say, and I can tell I caught him off guard.

He was probably expecting it to be a fight, but I know we need to figure this out and fast. Kingsley and I are supposed to leave for Hawaii in two days, and I need to figure out if that is still going to happen or if we'll be moving here.

"I'm out front," he says, and I start to pace around the room.

"Okay, room 216," I tell him.

"I'll be right there."

I text Kingsley and let her know that he's here to talk. She tells me to let her know if I need her. She'll stay away from the room until I text her again.

I pace back and forth, wringing my hands together. A

knock sounds at the door, and I stumble over my own feet as I head to answer it.

"Hi," I say shyly as I pull the door open.

"Hi, you look beautiful," he says as he comes into the hotel room.

"Thanks. You too."

I mean it. His dark brown hair is mussed, and he looks younger somehow. More vulnerable.

I can tell that he wants to reach for me, to pull me against him. I can almost see his wolf staring at me in his blue eyes, and I swallow hard.

Already I can feel my body warming. I sway towards him slightly before I can catch myself, and his eyes flash with heat.

"What did you want to talk about?" I ask him after a minute of us just staring at each other.

"About this morning. About you moving in with me," he says, and I nod.

"I wanted to talk about that too," I admit, and I see him swallow hard.

"You go first," he says, and I twist my fingers together in front of me.

"Okay, I ... it just feels like things are moving so fast. I can't deny that I have feelings for you, but it kind of feels like I'm the only one expected to give something up here. It's me moving to Aspen Ridge. Me leaving my family and friends. I'm giving up my home and support system. I'm giving up everything I've ever known, and I guess I just need some reassurance that this is forever."

"It is," he says right away, and I can see that he believes that. "We're fated to be together, Kaia."

"I know, but you grew up hearing that. You've known for your entire life that this was going to happen. I just found it out a few days ago. I'm still trying to get it straight in my head, I guess."

"I can give you time. I swear, Kaia, I'm going to prove it to you. I'll show you just how much I love you," he says, and my heart skips a beat in my chest.

"You love me?"

"Well, yeah. Of course, I do. You're my mate."

"I... you never said that before."

"I thought that it was obvious," he says.

I suppose that it was obvious to him. He smelled me and was instantly hooked. He knew right away that we were meant to be.

"Do you think that if you weren't a shifter you would still pick me?" I ask him quietly, and he swallows hard.

"I did pick you."

I frown, and he clears his throat.

"When I first met you and realized that you were my mate, I was anxious to actually claim you. After losing my parents, I just couldn't lose someone else, and you're more accident-prone than most."

"So, you weren't going to try to win me over or mark me?" I ask, my hand going to the bite mark on the base of my neck and shoulder.

"I told myself that I could choose. That I could live without you, but well, obviously, that didn't happen. I choose you, Kaia. I could never resist you. You make me laugh and smile more than anyone. I would have always fallen in love with you."

Tears sting the back of my eyes, and I know then that I'm in love with him too.

"I'll move wherever you want to go. If the choice is between you and this place and my pack, I would always choose you. Always," he promises me, and I nod.

"I love you, too."

He reaches for me then, pulling me flush against him, and I wrap my arms around him.

"I love you. I love you so much. I'll go anywhere that you are. I just need you to be happy. Just you."

I nod against him, a few tears slipping free, and I wipe them on his shirt. He laughs at the action, and I grin up at him.

"So... what now?" I ask him, and he grins down at me.

I have a feeling that I'm going to like what he has planned.

TEN

Micah

I HOLD Kaia's hand as we drive back to my house.

Our house, my wolf corrects me, and I smile to myself.

I haven't been able to stop touching her since she told me that she loved me too. Hearing her say those words just seemed to cement something inside of me. I haven't heard anyone tell me that in so long, and hearing my mate say it just seemed to fill a hole that I didn't even know was there.

Now I need to get her settled here in our home.

"I'll make some calls tomorrow to work on getting your things moved up here," I tell her as we pull into the driveway.

"I think that Kingsley and I will go home. I want to see our parents, and then we can go through what we want to move and what can be donated. Maybe you should come. You can meet the folks," she says as I turn the car off.

"Sounds good. I'll ask for time off tomorrow."

We climb out, and I take her hand in mine. As soon as I

touch her, that same pull becomes stronger. I glance at her, and I can tell that she's feeling it too.

I lead us inside and straight up the stairs. I can smell Kaia's arousal and hear her breathing pick up. She's just as turned on as I am.

As soon as we're in the bedroom, I pull her into my arms.

"I need you," I tell her, and my wolf starts to pace inside of me.

Kaia nods, her eyes filled with need, and I start to strip her clothes off slowly. I want to take my time with her tonight. I want to make love to her, to worship every inch of her. Already though, my animal is starting to push me to claim her faster.

I push down her pants and panties, bringing her underwear to my nose and breathing in her arousal. I growl, my wolf starting to push forward, and I hear Kaia moan.

"Micah," she begs, and I grin.

"You soaked these through, Kaia. Does that greedy pussy need my cock again, mate?"

She nods frantically as I prowl towards her, my intent clear in every step. She hits the edge of the bed and gasps as she tumbles backward. My cock hardens as I see her curves jiggle, and I pounce on her.

"I need you," I whisper against her skin a second before I bury my face in her drenched core.

I don't waste any time in licking her to an orgasm. I don't want to tease her today. I'm too far gone. I need to be inside of her. Now.

"Micah!" She shouts as she comes all over my face.

I lick up as much of her juices as I can. I love her sticky sweet taste, and my wolf is just as greedy for it.

"Oh god!" She moans, another orgasm rolling through

her, and I can't wait any longer. I stand, tearing at my clothes. I hear some of them rip, but I don't care. I need to be skin-on-skin with her. Now.

I spread her legs wide, my eyes meeting hers as I slam into her. She screams as I stretch her wide with my cock and push her further against the mattress.

HER TITS ARE hard pebbles pressed against my chest, and I love the feeling of them rubbing against me as I start to rut into her like the beast that I am.

Hearing her moan and scream my name already has me on edge. Feeling her tight little hole squeezing me so tight has my balls drawing up already, and I grit my teeth to stop from coming already. I need to get her off first.

"So damn hot," I growl as I pound into her.

My fingers find her clit, slipping over the dripping wet little bundle of nerves and I press down.

"Micah!" She screams and tingles start at the base of my spine.

I'm so close to coming and I grit my teeth.

"That's it. Give it to me, mate."

She cries out my name, her eyes meeting mine as she reaches her peak and I go flying over the edge with her.

ELEVEN

Kaia

FIVE YEARS LATER...

"THANKS AGAIN FOR WATCHING THEM," I tell Kingsley, and she laughs.

"Of course! I still owe you for babysitting for me the other week. Go have some fun with your man," she says with a smirk, and I grin.

"Oh, I will."

I wave goodbye to my kids, but they're too busy playing with their friends to really pay attention to me leaving. I'll see them bright and early tomorrow morning, so I wave to Kingsley and head back to my car.

Micah doesn't know it, but I have a surprise for him tonight. He's been working a lot these last few days, and I wanted us to have some alone time so I arranged for Kingsley to babysit overnight so Micah and I can connect.

There was an avalanche in a nearby town a week ago, and Micah left to help out. It was a small town, and they were struggling to keep up with all the patients. He has the next two days off now, and we're planning on having brunch with our friends tomorrow morning after we pick the kids up.

I make the short drive back to our cozy cabin and then hurry upstairs to our bedroom. Micah should be home soon, and I still need to get ready.

I strip off my clothes and take a quick shower. My phone rings as I'm toweling off, and I smile when I see my mom's name on the screen. My parents and Kingsley's parents just came to visit us last month, and I know they're itching to see us and their grandkids again soon.

They try to come see us or get us to go see them at least once a month. I love how they dote on our kids, and I know that Micah appreciates that they welcomed him into the family with open arms. He doesn't admit it, but I know he likes having a mother and father figure again.

The phone rings again, and I bite my lip. I don't have much time to get ready so I ignore the call. I'll have to call them back later.

I head into our closet, pull out the navy blue lace teddy, and slip it on. I'm just adjusting the straps when I hear the door open.

"Kaia, are you here, mate?" Micah calls.

"Upstairs!" I call back, grinning as I crawl onto the bed.

His heavy footsteps sound as he jogs up the stairs, and I push my hair behind my shoulder, thrusting my chest out as he rounds the corner and grinds to a halt in the doorway.

"Fuck me," he groans, and I grin.

"That was my line," I say seductively, and he grins.

"Where are the kids?" He whispers like they might hear him.

"At Kingsley and Asher's. All. Night. Long," I tell him.

"God, you're the best wife ever," he says, heading my way.

Micah and I got married about four months after I moved in with him. It seemed like every day I was falling more in love with him, and I knew then that this was forever for both of us.

We found out that we were pregnant two weeks after we said, 'I do.' I thought that Micah was the perfect mate and partner before, but once we learned that we were expecting, he really stepped it up.

He's been so supportive and attentive. He's the best dad and always makes time for the kids.

"I missed you so much," he says as he crawls up my body.

"I missed you more," I whisper as his lips land on mine.

We pull off Micah's clothes together, and his lips land on mine. His hands are all over my body, and just like every other time we make love, I can feel how much he needs me and how much he loves me with each touch.

"Micah...mate," I moan as he kisses his way down my neck.

His lips brush over my bite mark, and a baby orgasm rolls through me.

"Need to make sure you're nice and wet for what I have planned for tonight," he whispers huskily, and my breath catches at the hungry look in his eyes.

He kisses his way down my body, and I spread my legs for him greedily. He always knows just what to do to have me burning hot.

His tongue dips inside of me, and I fist the sheets as my orgasm starts to build inside of me.

"Mate," he whispers against my damp flesh, and there's something about the possessive tone in his voice that sends me over the edge.

I come hard, and before I can even come back down to earth, Micah is thrusting into me.

"I love you," I whisper, my hands running up his shoulders as I cling to him.

"I love you too," he says, his pace picking up.

I smile, my hips rising to meet his thrusts, and I know I'm in for one great night.

Looking for the rest of the Aspen Ridge Pack: Shifter M.D. series? Check them out here!

Bound To The Doctor
Bitten By The Doctor
Marked By The Doctor

Be sure to check out the Aspen Ridge Pack:
Loners
The Grizzlies Captive Mate

WANT A FREE BOOK?

Want a free copy of Wolf Lover? It's a steamy, scarred military hero, curvy girl romance! Check it out today here!

CONNECT WITH ME!

If you enjoyed this story, please consider leaving a review on Amazon or any other reader site or blog that you like. Don't forget to recommend it to your other reader friends.

If you want to chat with me, please consider joining my VIP list or connecting with me on one of my Social Media platforms. I love talking with each of my readers. Links below!

Website

9 798223 329145